This book must be returned by the date specified at the time of issue as
the DUE DATE FOR RETURN

The loan may be extended (personally, by post, telephone or online) for
a further period, if the book is not required by another reader, by quoting
the barcode / author / title.

Enquiries: 01709 336774

www.rotherham.gov.uk/libraries

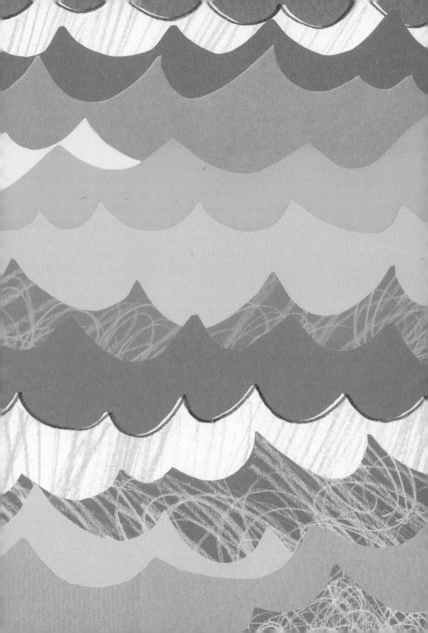

This book belongs to:

_____

to read with:

_____

MOLLY ROGERS TO THE RESCUE

Cornelia Funke

MOLLY ROGERS TO THE RESCUE

Illustrated by
Kasia Matyjaszek

Barrington Stoke

First published in 2019 in Great Britain by
Barrington Stoke Ltd
18 Walker Street, Edinburgh, EH3 7LP

www.barringtonstoke.co.uk

Text © 2019 Cornelia Funke
Illustrations © 2017 & 2019 Kasia Matyjaszek

The moral right of Cornelia Funke and Kasia Matyjaszek
to be identified as the author and illustrator of this work
has been asserted in accordance with the Copyright,
Designs and Patents Act, 1988

A CIP catalogue record for this book is available
from the British Library upon request

ISBN: 978-1-78112-839-8

Printed in China by Leo

This book is in a super-readable format for young readers
beginning their independent reading journey.

*For Lucan, with love
from Coleia*

Contents

Chapter 1
Pirate Work

Molly Rogers' mother was Barbarous Bertha.

She was the wildest pirate on the Seven Seas. Other pirates sobbed like babies when they heard her name.

But Barbarous Bertha was also the guardian of a wide stretch of emerald-green ocean and 23 islands.

The islands were called the Purple Shell Islands. Bertha and her crew protected the people who lived on them, and all the animals too.

She had taught Molly how to look after turtles and dolphins, and parrots and monkeys.

Each time Bertha chased leopard hunters or turtle-egg thieves, or pirates trying to plunder a village, Molly was there too. On board the fastest ship that sailed the oceans: the *Red Swallow*.

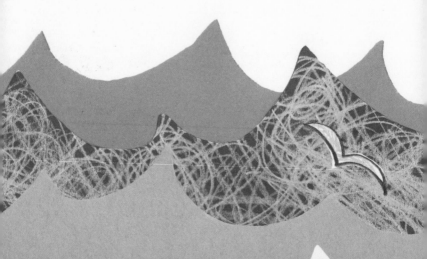

Chapter 2

Toothpick and Friends

One afternoon, Molly was on look-out duty when she saw a raft drifting on the ocean.

There were sharks all around it,
but the man on the raft was very skinny.
He wouldn't have made much of a meal
for half a shark.

He was holding an umbrella over
a very furry monkey and a turtle, and
two parrots were fanning them with
their wings.

"Tattoed Tammy!" Molly yelled. "Quick! It's Toothpick! I think he and his friends are in trouble!"

Toothpick lived on Monkey Skull Island, with 234 turtles, 87 parrots and 93 monkeys, and he knew all of them by name.

Toothpick liked animals better than people. And he liked to count them.

He counted the ones he didn't
know too:

3,667 beetles ...

36 snakes ...

It kept him rather busy.

Bertha rowed out to the raft with One-Eyed Wilma. Together, they chased the sharks away. Then they brought Toothpick and his friends back to the *Red Swallow*.

They ate a whole pot of Salty Sally's sea kelp soup and drank ten bottles of her pineapple pop before they told their story.

Chapter 3
Toothpick's Terrible Tale

What a terrible tale it was! The parrots did most of the talking, the monkey filled in bits in sign language, and Toothpick and the turtle added a sad sigh from time to time.

Molly was shocked to hear that a gang of pirates had taken over Monkey Skull Island. "But why are they digging up the whole island?" she asked.

"We have no idea!" the parrots croaked. Their names were Les and Lizzie.

"And they're chopping down the trees!" Lizzie screeched. "With our nests in them!"

"They ate three of the talking boars," Toothpick added with a deep sigh. "And there were only 12 of them to begin with. Their captain has a red beard. And his men are meaner than a swarm of bloodsucking mosquitoes. Right, Mumbles?"

Mumbles the monkey showed her teeth and shook her hairy fists, while the turtle, whose name was Erwin, hid in his shell.

"They call him Firebeard!" he moaned from inside his shell.

Molly looked at her mother. Firebeard was the name of the pirate who had kidnapped her once when she was on her way to visit her grandmother.

"Squid ink and whale spit!" Barbarous Bertha growled. "Firebeard! You were right, Molly! We should have left him and his men on Miserable Island with all the other rascals we caught. I was so glad to get you back in one piece that I was too soft on those scoundrels! Time to set that right!"

Chapter 4
Monkey Skull Island

It took the *Red Swallow* two days to reach Toothpick's home.

"Oh, I remember that island!"
Salty Sally said when they saw the three
green peaks of Monkey Skull Island on
the horizon. "Bloodhound Bill buried
his treasure here. Piles of jewels and
shiploads of English gold. Some say he
even stole two kings' crowns!"

"So that's what they are looking for!" Toothpick whispered. "If only they would find all those piles of gold and leave! We don't really need any treasure on our island, do we?"

Mumbles made a sign to show that she might like to try on a crown, but Erwin, Les and Lizzie just shook their heads.

Bertha and her crew landed their boats in a bay where the white sand was covered with singing shells. The shells began to hum softly when Molly stepped on one. She loved that sound.

"Where did Firebeard anchor his ship?" Tattooed Tammy asked.

Mumbles pointed a furry finger to the west of the island.

"Well, my love," Barbarous Bertha said to Molly. "I think it's time to call that friend of yours!"

Molly closed her fingers around the whistle she wore around her neck and smiled.

Chapter 5
Eight – the Kraken

The singing shells were still humming when Molly stepped into the waves that licked over the beach of Monkey Skull Island.

She drew a deep breath, dipped the whistle into the water and blew into it as hard as she could.

"You'd better all step back!" called Salty Sally.

She sounded so serious that even Erwin the turtle did what she said.

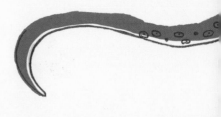

And here he was! A HUGE Kraken rose from the ocean, waving at Molly and Bertha with three of his eight arms.

"Eight!" Molly called up to him. "Please can you swim to the ship that's anchored west of this island? Grab any pirates on board and make sure it doesn't leave!"

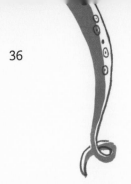

The Kraken rolled four arms to show that he'd do what Molly asked. Then he sank back into the ocean and showered everyone on the beach with water.

"By Neptune's green toenails, Bertha!" said Toothpick. "Your daughter's got some truly great friends."

Then he put Erwin under his arm and led the crew of the *Red Swallow* further into the island, towards the noises of swearing and shovelling that were coming from the jungle.

Chapter 6
Firebeard

Through the trees, they soon saw the clearing the pirates had chopped into the jungle.

Yes. There they were, the pirates Molly remembered so well.

Morgan O'Meany, Firebeard's
helmsman; the ship's cook, Cutlass Tom;
Billy the Bald; William Wooden Hand;

Crooked Carl and the rest of the
motley bunch. As well as, of course,
their captain, Firebeard.

"Shark blood and sardine stink!" Captain Firebeard yelled, and threw a shovel of dirt at Billy the Bald. "That map lies better than I do! We've dug more holes in the ground than there are moth holes in your shirt. And not a single gold coin!"

"Why don't we just blow up this whole rotten island?" Crooked Carl growled. "We've got enough dynamite!"

"Yes!" the others yelled. "Let's blow it up!"

And the jungle roared with pirate laughter.

Toothpick and his friends looked at
Bertha in alarm. The island was their
home!

But Bertha just smiled.

"Don't worry. Molly has a plan
and you all have a part to play," she
whispered. Then she turned to her crew.
"Sally, get him ready!" she cried.

Toothpick's eyes grew wide as Salty Sally took out the pirate ketchup and smeared it all over his face and clothes.

Then Molly explained her plan and Toothpick began to smile from ear to ear.

Chapter 7

Molly's Marvellous Plan

Toothpick truly looked like a man covered in his own blood when he stumbled into the clearing. And he smelled just a little bit of ketchup.

"Cannibaaaaaaals!" he screamed, shaking his red hands at the pirates. "Run for your lives! For Neptune's sake! Cannibaaaaaals!"

The trees around the clearing began to shake.

Roars and shrill screams filled the jungle.

Mumbles and all her relatives had climbed into the branches. They shouted swear words in every language that had ever been heard on the island.

High above them swarms of parrots added to the noise.

No one could imitate leopards, wild boars and swearing pirates better than the parrots of Monkey Skull Island.

And there were 87 of them!

Captain Firebeard was the first
to run.

The others dropped their shovels and
followed him.

They made straight for the beach where they'd left their boats. But when they stumbled out of the jungle, they all froze.

A girl was standing on the beach. And she looked very familiar.

"Hello, Firebeard!" Molly said with a grin. "I think you might remember me?"

"Yes, surprise, surprise!" cried Barbarous Bertha as she stepped up to stand beside her daughter.

Firebeard stumbled back and fell over a turtle.

There were lots of turtles in the sand. In fact, the whole beach was covered with them. Erwin had a lot of friends.

Chapter 8
The Broken Promise

"I thought you'd promised that you'd become a coconut trader if we let you go?" said Barbarous Bertha.

"No proper pirate ever keeps his promises!" Firebeard growled. "And especially not when it's to a bunch of women and a little girl!"

He drew his sword and waved at his men. "Come on! Let's make mincemeat of them!"

But before the pirates could grab their swords, two dozen lassos flew out of the jungle and wrapped the pirates up like spring rolls.

Molly had to stop the monkeys from beating their prisoners up too badly, but she did let the turtles march all over them, and the parrots got permission to pull their hair.

Then she called Eight, who already
held some of the pirates in his arms.

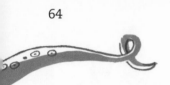

Firebeard and his men wiggled like sardines when the Kraken picked them out of the sand like pebbles.

He carried them all back to the *Red Swallow*, and when Molly and Bertha arrived, Eight had already piled the pirates on the deck like sacks of coffee beans.

"Thank you so much, Eight!" Molly called up to him. Then she frowned.

The Kraken was pointing at something with his arms. He looked quite upset.

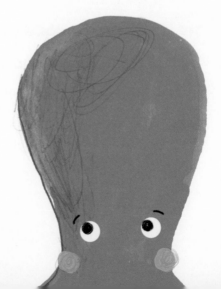

"What's he trying to tell us?" Bertha asked.

Molly frowned and her face grew red with anger.

"He says there are six children on board the *Horrible Haddock*. All tied up. They were scared of Eight, so he left them where they were."

Chapter 9
Bertha's Fury

Bertha's face went as red as a poppy.

"Six children?" she said. "Six children tied up as prisoners on board the *Horrible Haddock*?"

Bertha turned to Molly. "Get them, Molly!" she cried.

But Molly had already jumped back into the rowing boat and was on her way.

While she rowed over to the *Horrible Haddock*, her mother went to see Firebeard.

"You child-stealing, tree-chopping, all-in-all disgusting tick of a man!" Bertha shouted. "Tell me where you stole those children from right now, or I'll feed you to the Kraken myself!"

"OK, OK, I'll tell you!" growled Firebeard. "They're all fine! No reason to get upset!"

And then he swore by his beard
and all the gold he'd stolen in his long
pirate life that he'd never again kidnap
children, or kill talking boars, or dig up
islands for treasure.

But this time it was no good. Bertha
showed no mercy.

Chapter 10

Firebeard's New Home

Eight enjoyed himself. While all the children watched, he dropped Firebeard and his men on a bare and empty rock in the middle of the sea. Miserable Island was a good name for it.

"There's a cactus on the island with fruit you can eat!" Molly called over to the pirates. "It doesn't taste very nice and it's quite prickly. But it's better than any of the food we ever got from you!"

"I'll get my revenge, Molly Rogers!" Firebeard yelled. "Just you wait! And next time I catch you, I'll feed you to the sharks!"

"I look forward to it!" Molly called back.

Then she and Barbarous Bertha took the kidnapped children back to their parents.

But two of them wanted to stay on board the *Red Swallow*.

Of course they did. Who wouldn't
want to be friends with turtles and
krakens and chase child-snatching
pirates like Firebeard?

Our books are tested
for children and young people by
children and young people.

Thanks to everyone who consulted on
a manuscript for their time and effort in
helping us to make our books better
for our readers.